NEW YORK TIMES BESTSELLING AUTHOR

Rachel Held Evans and Matthew Paul Turner

What Is GOD Like?

ILLUSTRATIONS BY YING HUI TAN

CONVERGENT

Foreword

Woven throughout this book, you'll find Rachel's heart for people, love of words, and the solace she discovered in the unknown.

It was March of 2019 when she started outlining and writing drafts of children's books. As new parents, Rachel and I were in a fresh chapter of life. Our son, Henry, had just turned three, and our daughter, Harper, was still a baby. Rachel was excited to write stories they could enjoy. We had big plans and were building a house.

But the crushing reality is that life doesn't always go according to our plans. Rachel wasn't able to finish the ideas for all her books. She got sick in April and passed away on May 4, 2019, two weeks before Harper's first birthday.

Matthew Paul Turner was often with me at Rachel's hospital bedside in the days before her death. His personal connection to Rachel and her words permeates the poetic fabric of art and text that you now hold. It's an honor to work with Matthew, who has championed Rachel and her work from the beginning of her career, before *New York Times* bestseller lists, before media appearances, and before he was known as a children's book author.

It's also a privilege to work with Ying Hui Tan, who ensures with breathtaking beauty that the ideas of Rachel and Matthew are seen. I'm grateful to Rachel, Ying Hui, Matthew, and the team at Convergent for their hard work. And I'm excited to share the collaboration of these artists with you.

We are all fellow travelers through this life. Together, we learn to care for one another. Join me in these pages to discover ancient imagery, history, love, dedication to what's good, and acceptance of all people. Together, we wonder how we're simultaneously insignificant and grand in this vast universe. Together, let's explore the question:

What is God like?

—Daniel Jonce Evans

What is GOD like?

That's a **very big question**, one that people from places all around the world have wondered about since the beginning of time.

And while nobody has seen all of God (because God is far too big for any of us to fully see),

we can know what God is like.

God is like an eagle, sharp eyed and swift, with wings so wide you can play under their shadows.

God is like a river, constant and life giving. When you grow near God, you'll sprout up strong as a tree.

God is like the stars, forever present and bright. Even when they feel far away, you can always look up and see them winking at you.

God is like a shepherd, brave and good, a protector who loves her sheep so much that she watches over all of them and knows each of their names by heart.

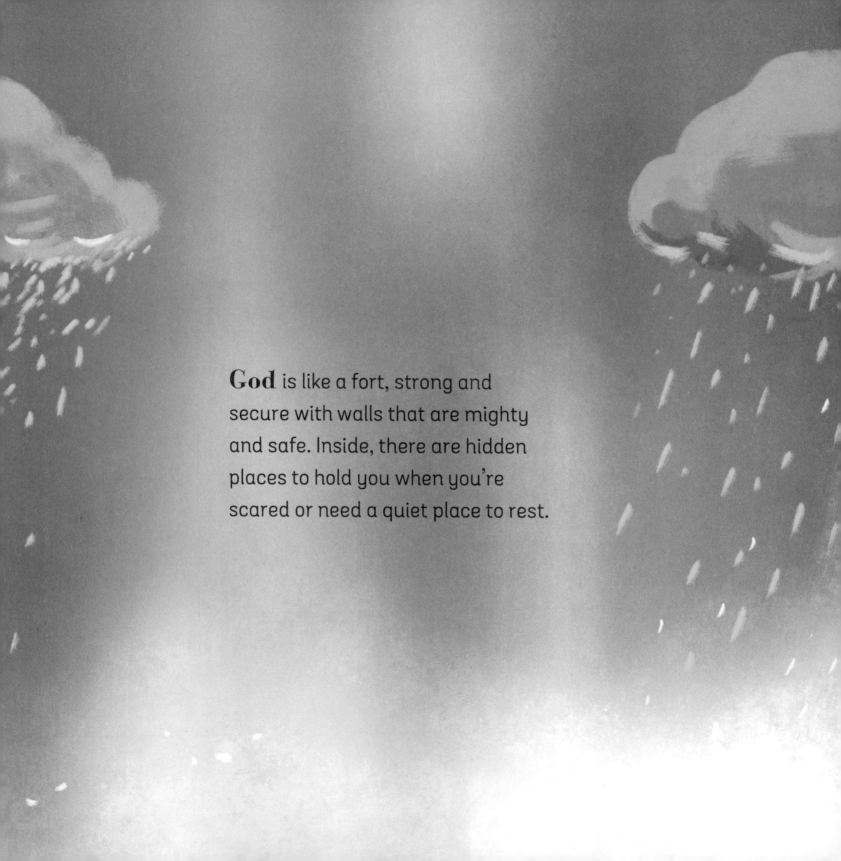

God is like a fort, strong and
secure with walls that are mighty
and safe. Inside, there are hidden
places to hold you when you're
scared or need a quiet place to rest.

God is like a gardener, patient and nurturing.

God plants, waters, weeds, and fertilizes the earth until every good thing on it seeks the nourishing sun and grows.

God is like the flame of a candle,
warm and inviting.

With **God** close by, you can look to the
light and see through the darkest of nights.

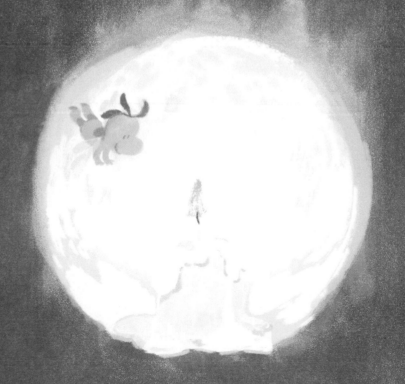

God is like the wind, passionate and full of mystery.

God is both here and, mysteriously, also over there.

God is everywhere, swirling throughout the world, whistling across mountain ranges, rustling through trees, and pressing against your cheeks on a breezy day.

God is like an artist, creative and unpredictable, always busy making and remaking everything brilliant and new.

God is like a mother, strong and safe.

You can crawl up into her lap whenever you want to, and she will hold you until you fall asleep.

God is like a father, gentle and safe. He will put you on top of his shoulders to give you a bird's-eye view of all creation.

God is like three dancers, graceful and precise.

They move to the same music in very different ways, showcasing all of God's elegance and rhythm in your life.

God is like a rainbow, vivid and full of color, a dazzling reminder of promise and hope for all people after a storm.

God is like a best friend, faithful and true, closer to you than even your brothers or sisters.

And because we know what **God** is like, we know that . . .

God is kind.

God is forgiving.

God is slow to get angry.

God is quick to be glad.

God is happy when you tell the truth
and sad when things are unfair.

She is your protector.

He is trustworthy.

They are friends when you feel alone.

God hopes. **God** perseveres.

What is **God** like?

That's a **very big question**, one that people from places all around the world, throughout all time, have answered in many different ways. Keep searching. Keep wondering. Keep learning about God.

But whenever you aren't sure what God is like, think about what makes you feel safe, what makes you feel brave, and what makes you feel loved.

That's what God is like.

For Henry and Harper.

May you find comfort in mystery.

Copyright © 2021 by Rachel Held Evans and Daniel Jonce Evans
Illustrations copyright © 2021 by Ying Hui Tan

Published in the United States by Convergent Books, an imprint of Random House, a division of Penguin Random House LLC.

Convergent Books is a registered trademark, and its C colophon is a trademark of Penguin Random House LLC.

Thank you, Sarah Bessey, Jeff Chu, and Cindy Brandt, for helping bring this book to life.

ISBN 978-0-593-19331-0
Ebook ISBN 978-0-593-19332-7

Library of Congress Cataloging-in-Publication Data
Names: Evans, Rachel Held, 1981–2019, author. | Turner, Matthew Paul, 1973– author. | Tan, Ying Hui, illustrator.
Title: What is God Like? / by Rachel Held Evans and Matthew Paul Turner ; illustrations by Ying Hui Tan.
Description: First edition. | New York : Convergent Books, [2021]
Identifiers: LCCN 2020041544 | ISBN 9780593193310 | ISBN 9780593193327 (ebook)
Subjects: LCSH: God (Christianity)—Juvenile literature. | God (Christianity)—Art—Juvenile literature.
Classification: LCC BT107 .E93 2021 | DDC 231—dc23
LC record available at https://lccn.loc.gov/2020041544.

Printed in the United States of America

convergentbooks.com

10 9 8 7 6 5 4 3 2 1

First Edition

Book design by Sonia Persad
Cover design by Stephanie Huntwork and Jan Derevjanik
Cover illustrations by Ying Hui Tan